T0144949

The Amazing Journey of Solomon

Pamela Cannalte

Illustrated by Steven Beutler
Designed by Jody Mattics

The Sockeye Salmon

SB

AuthorHouse™
1663 Liberty Drive
Bloomington, IN 47403
www.authorhouse.com
Phone: 1 (800) 839-8640

Published by AuthorHouse 12/26/2018

ISBN: 978-1-5462-7356-1 (sc)
ISBN: 978-1-5462-7355-4 (hc)
ISBN: 978-1-5462-7357-8 (e)

Library of Congress Control Number: 2018915051

Print information available on the last page.

Any people depicted in stock imagery provided by Getty Images are models,
and such images are being used for illustrative purposes only.
Certain stock imagery © Getty Images.

This book is printed on acid-free paper.

Because of the dynamic nature of the Internet, any web addresses or links contained in this book may have changed
since publication and may no longer be valid. The views expressed in this work are solely those of the author and do not
necessarily reflect the views of the publisher, and the publisher hereby disclaims any responsibility for them.

authorHOUSE®

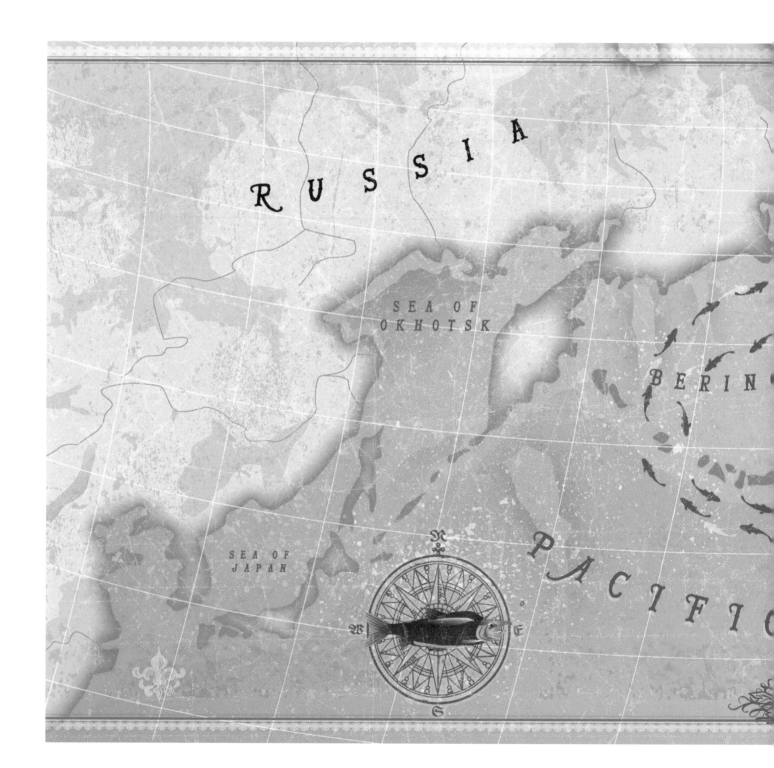

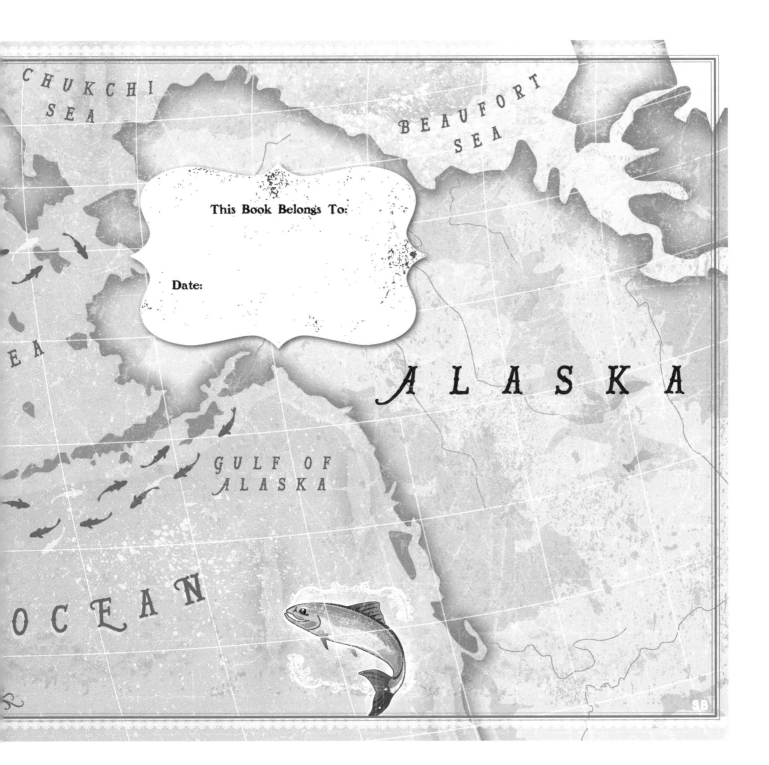

This Book Belongs To:

Date:

The Amazing Journey of Solomon

The Sockeye Salmon

The Amazing Journey
of Solomon
The Sockeye Salmon

Copyright 2014

First Edition 2016

ISBN: 978-0-9758812-9-3

DoubleShoe Publishing
Highway 550 South
Montrose, CO

Author:
Pamela Cannalte
Ridgway, CO
pamelacannalte@yahoo.com

Illustration:
Steven Beutler
Montrose, CO
art@stevenbeutlerdesign.com

Design:
Jody Mattics
Montrose, CO
jmattics@me.com

~ About the Creators of this Book ~

Pamela Cannalte

Pamela was born in New Jersey and grew up in Tucson, Arizona. She attended the University of Arizona. After years of working in both the corporate technical and creative worlds, she has returned to teaching and writing. Pamela has two amazing children, a son who lives in Hawaii and a daughter who lives in Alaska, and is blessed with four beautiful grandchildren, who have been the inspiration for her books. She has lived in many places across the country, one of her favorite being Eagle River, Alaska. Pamela now resides just outside of the quaint town of Ridgway, in the San Juan Mountains of Southwestern Colorado.

Steven Beutler

Steven is an award winning illustrator and graphic designer. His client list boasts of names such as Hallmark Cards, Sprint, The Kansas City Star and Little Yellow Bicycle. He owns and operates a illustration and graphic design company in Western Colorado. When he is not being a perfectionist, you can usually find him on the slopes of Telluride as a part time ski instructor. See more of his work at www.stevenbeutlerdesign.com.

Jody Mattics

A Western Colorado native, Jody is a gifted graphic designer with an admirable work ethic and a delicious sense of humor. The quality of her design and layout work on previous book projects has received numerous compliments from national book award judges as well as an untold number of readers. She is a joy to work with due to her patience and ability, always with a smile, to accommodate requests and changes. Her biggest accomplishments are raising two young men of which she is most proud.

Little *Solomon* came from the headwaters of the Russian River on the Kenai Peninsula in Southwest Alaska. He and his siblings were hatched from tiny pink colored eggs, about the size of a pencil eraser, placed by their parents in gravel nests at the bottom of the stream.

Their birth place was surrounded by a vast, beautiful spruce forest and towering snowcapped peaks.

Solomon and his brothers and sisters hatched about three months after their mother laid her eggs in the crystal clear, icy water that came down from the glaciers, which hung from the nearby high mountain valleys.

Look closely; can you find how many animals live in this Alaskan high mountain valley?

Once hatched, *Solomon* looked at his brothers and sisters and was amused by their appearance; however, he then realized he looked just like them. They were all about one inch in length, and Solomon thought they all looked very strange, with extremely huge eyes and large bellies which contained egg yolks.

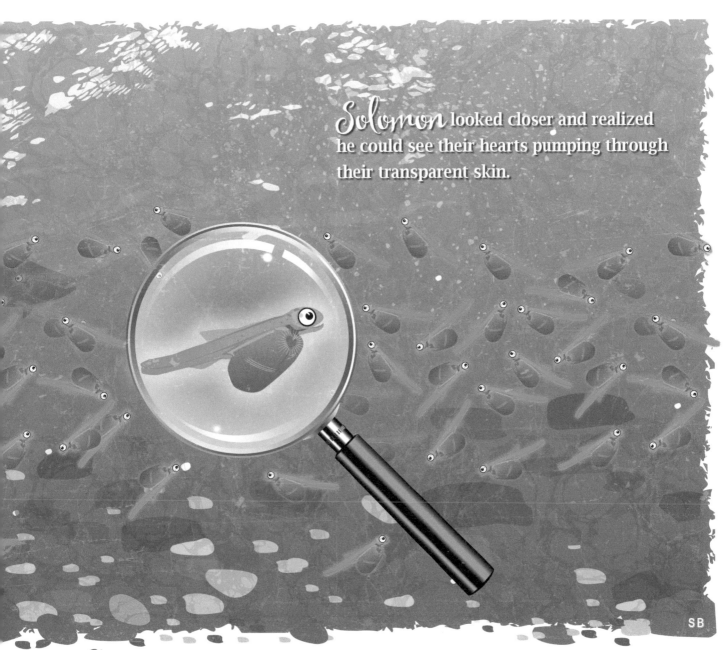

Solomon looked closer and realized he could see their hearts pumping through their transparent skin.

Look closely; Solomon has a large family. Can you count how many brothers and sisters he has?

As days ran into weeks, *Solomon* and his siblings remained hidden in the gravel, living off their egg sacs. Slowly they were using up all of their yolks, and their bellies shrank and then totally disappeared. As baby salmon, they were getting very hungry, and so began leaving their gravel nests in search of the food they needed to survive.

Look closely; Solomon has become very hungry. Can you find what he is having for lunch?

Solomon ate anything and everything that went floating by in the stream, but he especially enjoyed insects, which were his favorite.

Very soon the young, vulnerable salmon realized they all must be extremely cautious in the crystal clear water, as there were frogs, birds, eagles, other much larger fish, bears and other mammals, all in search of a delicious meal of baby salmon! Solomon was always on the lookout for danger.

Look closely; can you find how many creatures might want to eat Solomon for lunch?

Little *Solomon* knew it was time to begin their long journey downstream to the sea, which would take a couple of years. They had traveled far enough down the Russian River to where it joins the Kenai River, to realize, by instinct, that the water had become wide and very fast moving.

Not only must he and his brothers and sisters find food to survive, but they also needed to hide under big rocks and among the plants in the river to avoid all of the predators they would encounter on this difficult trip swimming downstream to the ocean. But Solomon's parents had passed down to them the ability to camouflage themselves among the rocks and vegetation in the river, giving the young salmon beautiful bars and spots on their bodies, which served to hide them very well.

SB

Look closely; Solomon's brothers and sisters are good at hide and seek. Can you find all of their hiding spots?

The amazing journey continued; *Solomon* was now three years old and ready to venture out into the Bering Sea. Solomon and his siblings had become restless for travel. Solomon was no longer little, nor was he the same color as he was in the stream. He lost the markings and spots on his body and had turned slightly blue-tinged, bright and silvery in color. And unlike their cousins, Solomon and his sockeye family did not have a spot on their tail or back.

 Solomon was also aware that his body was adjusting to the change from the fresh water of the river, to the saltwater of the sea.

Look closely; can you find the new salt water creatures that Solomon and his family discover?

At first, they all stayed close to the shore, feeding on mostly insects and plankton, but slowly moved farther out into the sea. *Solomon* knew their ocean journey would be long and hazardous. The "school" of beautiful salmon had to be aware of the fact that there were many more dangers in the open water than in the river. They were hunted by otters, sea lions, orca whales, and their most dangerous predator: fishermen! Some fishermen used large nets, which would easily snag the gills of the beautiful fish.

SB

 Look closely; can you find which creature in these Alaskan waters eats the most Salmon?

Solomon knew intuitively that his migration was taking him on more than a 2,000-mile journey.

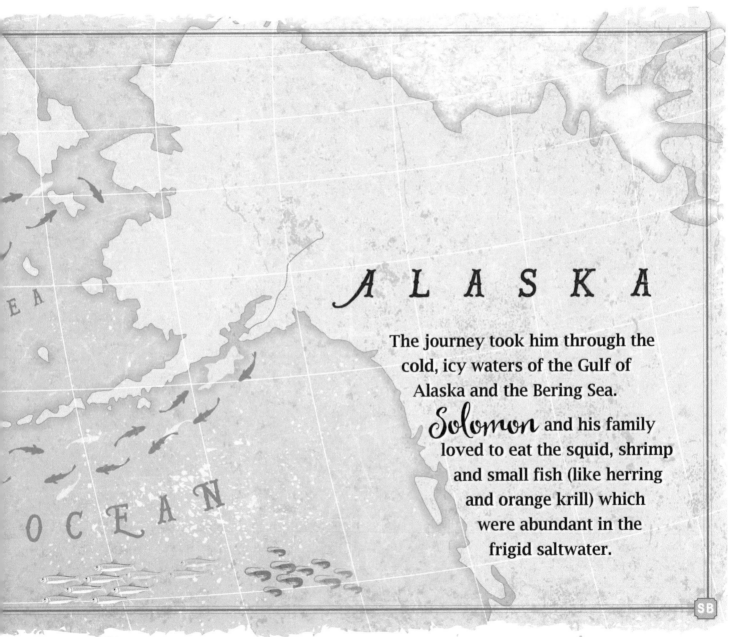

EA

A L A S K A

The journey took him through the cold, icy waters of the Gulf of Alaska and the Bering Sea.

Solomon and his family loved to eat the squid, shrimp and small fish (like herring and orange krill) which were abundant in the frigid saltwater.

OCEAN

SB

Look closely; can you find which direction Solomon needs to swim to get back home?

Solomon's amazing journey in the ocean continued for three more years before he began his trip back to his original birthplace to spawn. Solomon knew exactly where his birth river was, the headwaters of the Russian River. He felt his body re-adapting to the fresh water. Most of his siblings were by his side, but their bodies, like Solomon's, were changing also. Their bodies were all beginning to turn red and their heads were turning green.

SB

Look closely; Solomon's brothers and sisters look very much alike, but are different. Can you spot the differences?

Solomon and his siblings began their challenging journey back to the stream where they were born. They did not have to eat any longer; they lived on the fat within their bodies. Swimming vigorously upstream against rugged rapids, leaping over rocky waterfalls, Solomon and his family also had to traverse fish ladders, avoid fishermen's nets and hooks, and stay away from hungry bears and eagles.

Look closely; can you count how many bears came to the river to eat dinner?

After days of swimming, Solomon
and his brothers and sisters finally
reached their birth stream, exhausted,
but ready to have babies of their own, as
Solomon's parents had done before him.

Solomon had found a mate, and watched as she carefully cleared a spot in the streambed by sweeping her tail back and forth, thereby creating a gravel nest. Solomon swam back and forth and around her as she laid her eggs in the gravel nest. She swam a short distance from the nest, looking back towards Solomon.

SB

Look closely; can you count how many eggs Solomon's mate has layed in her nest?

He KNEW **IT WAS** HIS **TURN** *to* SWIM **OVER** THE EGGS **AND** FERTILIZE them.

Solomon WAS **UNBELIEVABLY** protective of THE fertilized EGGS **FOR** two weeks.

Solomon's AMAZING JOURNEY **WAS** coming TO an end, but **AT** THE **SAME** TIME, his LEGACY was just beginning. **LIFE** WAS beautifully starting **OVER** WITH THE BIRTH **OF** his offspring.

Look closely; can you find the other animal couples that live in this beautiful Alaskan landscape?

Glossary of Terms

From Merriam-Webster Dictionary

Headwaters: the source of a stream

Siblings: a brother or sister

Gravel: small pieces of rock

Vast: very great in size, amount, or extent

Glacier: a very large area of ice that moves slowly down a slope or valley or over a wide area of land

Transparent: able to be seen through

Vulnerable: open to attack, harm, or damage

Cautious: careful about avoiding danger or risk

Journey: an act of traveling from one place to another

Predators: an animal that lives by killing and eating other animals: an animal that preys on other animals

Camouflage: something (such as color or shape) that protects an animal from attack by making the animal difficult to see in the area around it

Plankton: the very small animal and plant life in an ocean, lake, etc.

Hazardous: involving risk or danger

"School": any group of fish that stay together

Intuitively: having the ability to know or understand things without any proof or evidence: having or characterized by intuition

Migration: to move from one area to another at different times of the year

Orange krill: very small creatures in the ocean that salmon eat

Birthplace: place of birth or origin

Spawn: to produce or lay eggs in water

Challenging: difficult in a way

Fish Ladder: a series of pools built like steps to enable fish to bypass a dam or waterfall

Streambed: the channel occupied or formerly occupied by a stream

Fertilize: to make (an egg) able to grow and develop

Legacy: something transmitted by or received from an ancestor or predecessor or from the past

Offspring: the product of the reproductive processes of an animal or plant

SB

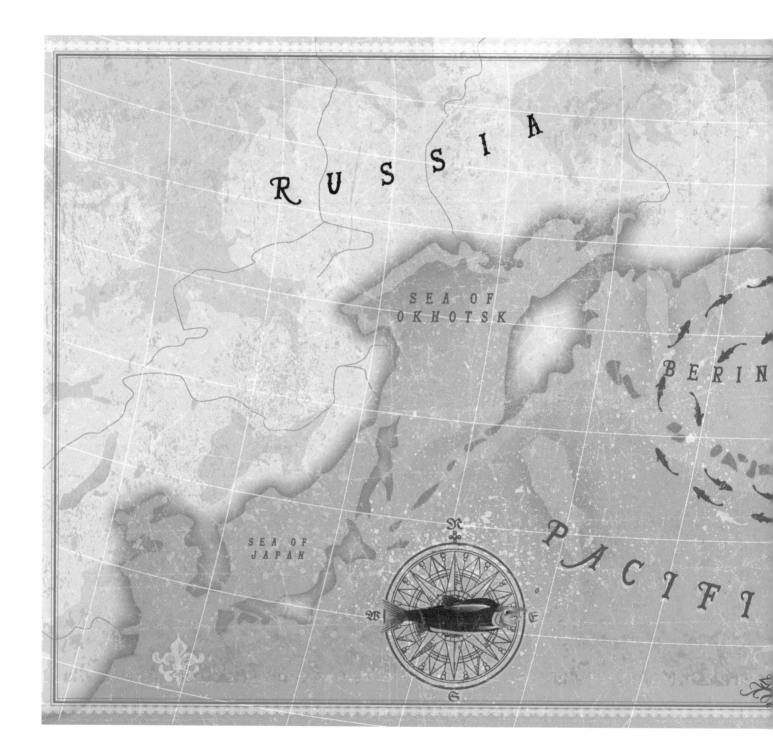

Life Stages of the Alaskan Sockeye Salmon

Eggs
hatch in about
3 months.

Alevin
Feeds off of yolk-sac
for several weeks.

Spawning Adult
Spawn and die within
2 weeks.

Fry
5 to 10 weeks old
and swimming.

Parr
Several months old,
develops "finger"
markings

Adult
Spends 1-8 years
at sea.

Smolt
1-3 years old.
Will group and head
out to sea.

Printed in the United States
By Bookmasters